DIF
FER
EN

love > hate

Dedicated to the memory of Sharonda Coleman-Singleton and Christopher Robin Singleton

Designed by David Miles

Paperback ISBN: 978-1-7350827-1-4
Hardcover ISBN: 978-1-7350827-0-7

First Edition

Printed in the United States

10 9 8 7 6 5 4 3 2 1

DIF FER EN

A STORY ABOUT
LOVING YOUR
NEIGHBOR

CHRIS
SINGLETON

ILLUSTRATIONS BY
WILIAM
LUONG

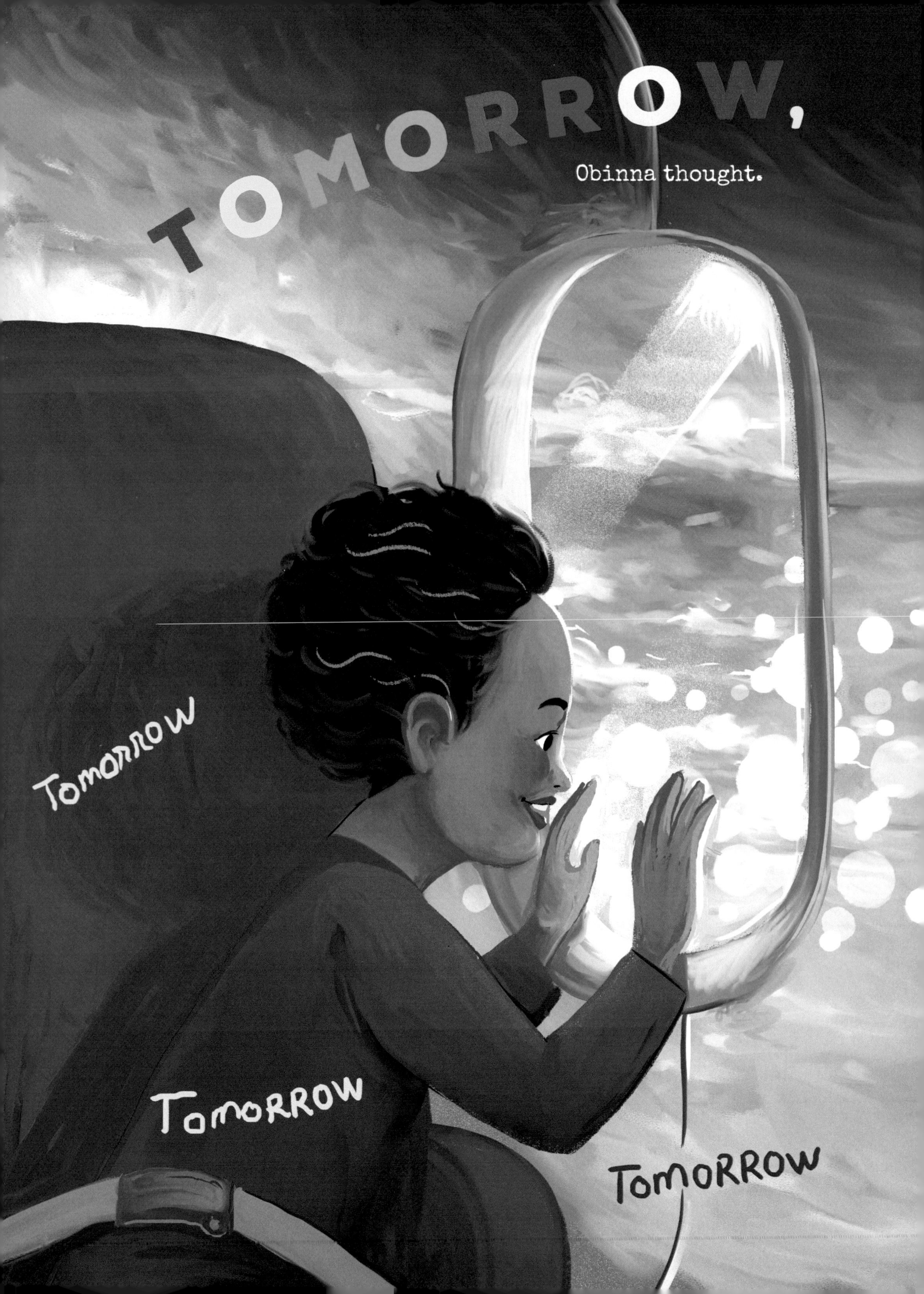

TOMORROW,

Obinna thought.

Tomorrow

Tomorrow

Tomorrow

Obinna had thought about it on the plane all the way from
Nigeria. He'd thought about it while people in uniforms
stamped his parents' paperwork. He'd thought about it
during the long, hot car ride to Charleston. Now they were
finally here, and so was tomorrow—the first day of school.

He carefully smoothed
the front of his
dashiki. Obinna loved
his traditional clothes.
They took him back
home, back to Nigeria.

The reds were like the setting sun, crimson behind the mountains. The golds glimmered like the dancing grasses of the savanna. The blues shone like the endless depths of the warm, living ocean. *Tomorrow*, he thought. *Tomorrow he would show all his classmates what it was to be Nigerian.*

The next morning, Obinna gulped down his breakfast and rushed out the door, his sneakers pounding the sidewalk. *Pound, pound, pound.*

pound   pound   pound

He ran past the neighbors, around the corner store, toward the school gates . . .

. . . and
straight into
Mrs. Sharonda.

"Careful, sugarfoot!" cried Mrs. Sharonda. But then she smiled. "You're a strong runner, as long as you look where you're going," she said with a wink. "New student? I believe you're in my class right over here."

The classroom was noisy, like classrooms usually
are at the beginning of a school day. But when Obinna
walked in, there was a sudden, uncomfortable silence.
Twenty students were already in the room, and twenty
pairs of eyes took in Obinna's clothing, his hair—
his *difference*. Then twenty people started laughing.

"Look at his clothes!" said one boy.

"I would never wear *that* to school," said a girl.

"And where did he get that haircut?" laughed another.

"Hush now," said Mrs. Sharonda. But it was too late.

Obinna burst out of the room and ran. *Pound, pound, pound.* Through the hallway, past the office, around the corner, into the bathroom he ran, his tears mingling with his sneakers on the tile floor.

He pulled off his dashiki and threw it on the ground. *Yesterday,* Obinna cried. *Oh, how I wish it was yesterday instead.*

He cried for Nigeria. He cried for the sun and the savanna and the ocean. He cried to be normal. But he couldn't. He was different. Different like his dashiki.

There was a knock on the door.
"Obinna?" It was Mrs. Sharonda.
Obinna wiped his eyes, sniffed, and went out to his teacher.
She handed him a tissue. Her eyes were soft, the kind of eyes that seem to know exactly what you're feeling without you having to say a word. They sat in silence for a long time. Then,
"Never be ashamed of who you are, Obinna," Mrs. Sharonda said. "You are beautifully and wonderfully made."

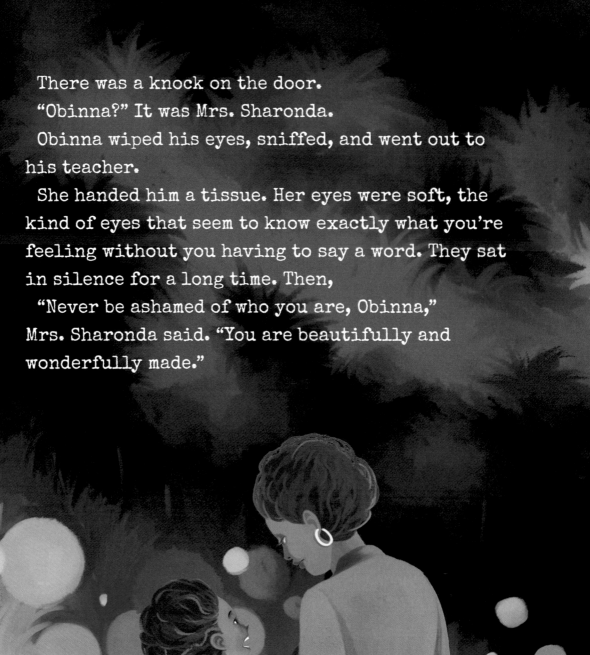

"I'm not," Obinna said. "I'll never fit in."

"But I think that you, Obinna, weren't made to fit in," Mrs. Sharonda said. "You were made to stand out. You'll see."

She gave Obinna a hug and helped him put his dashiki back on. "And," she said, "I think our class will need your help in the school relay race. I haven't seen a boy run like you in all my years of teaching. How about we join the class on the field?"

All the classes from the school were lined up along the field outside. Obinna's class hooped and hollered with excitement, but Obinna snuck to the back of the line, his hands deep in his pockets as if he could pull himself in and hide. Yesterday, he thought to himself.

The principal stood at the edge of the field. "At the sound of the whistle, each class must have one student run the length of the field and return to the line," he said. "He or she must tag the next student, and they must run the field as well. The first class to have all students finish will be the winner. Ready? Three, two, one—"

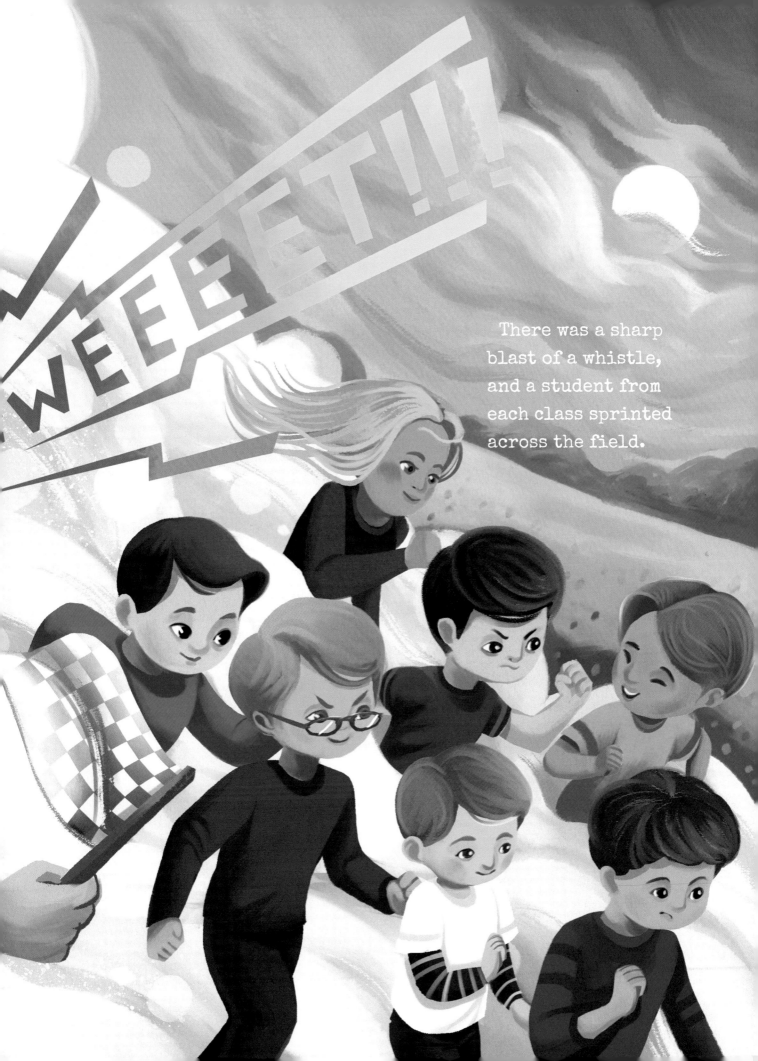

There was a sharp blast of a whistle, and a student from each class sprinted across the field.

Obinna couldn't help cheering with the rest of his class. The first student finished, and with Obinna in line, there were twenty students left. Then fifteen. Then ten. Then five!

Obinna's class was tied for first with another class. *Three students left!* Still tied. *Two students left!* The other class was pulling ahead. *One student left!*

And then Obinna realized
it was his turn.

He slammed his sneakers into the grass. *Pound, pound, pound.* He pumped his arms. He rocketed across the field.

"Go Obinna!" cheered Mrs. Sharonda.

"GO OBINNA!" screamed his class. In the excitement of the race, it seemed everything else was forgotten. His difference, his hair, his dashiki blowing furiously in the wind.

Pound

Pound

Pound pound

Pound

Pound

He made it all the way to the end of the field and turned around for the final length. The other class's last runner was a little way ahead of him. Obinna put on a burst of speed and raced across the field. *Pound, pound, pound.* He ran past the half marker, past the quarter marker, past the end—and straight into the arms of his cheering classmates.

"Mrs. Sharonda's class wins!" said the principal.

Mrs. Sharonda's class screamed and cheered and lifted Obinna into their arms—dashiki and all.

They marched back to class, this time with Obinna at the front of the line. And as the excitement died down, some of Obinna's classmates seemed to remember that Obinna was different. They saw his hair. They took in his dashiki. But this time . . .

"I'm sorry, Obinna," said one boy.
"Me too," said a girl.
"I think what you're wearing is pretty neat," said another. "Is that from where you're from?"
Obinna grinned. He told them about the crimson sun. He described the golden savanna and the blue oceans. The class was amazed.

"Mrs. Sharonda," they said, "Can we learn more about Nigeria?"
Obinna smiled to himself.

TODAY,

he thought. *Today is the best day ever.*

DISCUSSION QUESTIONS

1 Why do you think Obinna's classmates had a hard time accepting him at first?

2 Have you ever met someone that seemed different from you? Did you have similar feelings?

3 What seemed to change the minds of Obinna's classmates? What can we learn from their example?

4 Imagine that you moved to a new city where people act and speak and dress differently than you. How would you feel? How does that help you imagine how other people in that situation might feel?

5 Can people choose where they're from or what they look like? What does that mean for how we should treat them?

6 Mrs. Sharonda told Obinna that he was made to stand out. In fact, all of us are made to stand out in one way or another. What special differences do you have that make you stand out?

7 What would the world be like if we were all the same? How is it helpful that we have unique differences?